E R R A T A

The labels on the planet signs on pages 28-29 are incorrect.
From left to right the signs should read:
PLUTO, NEPTUNE, URANUS, SATURN, JUPITER . . . .

This will be corrected in subsequent printings.

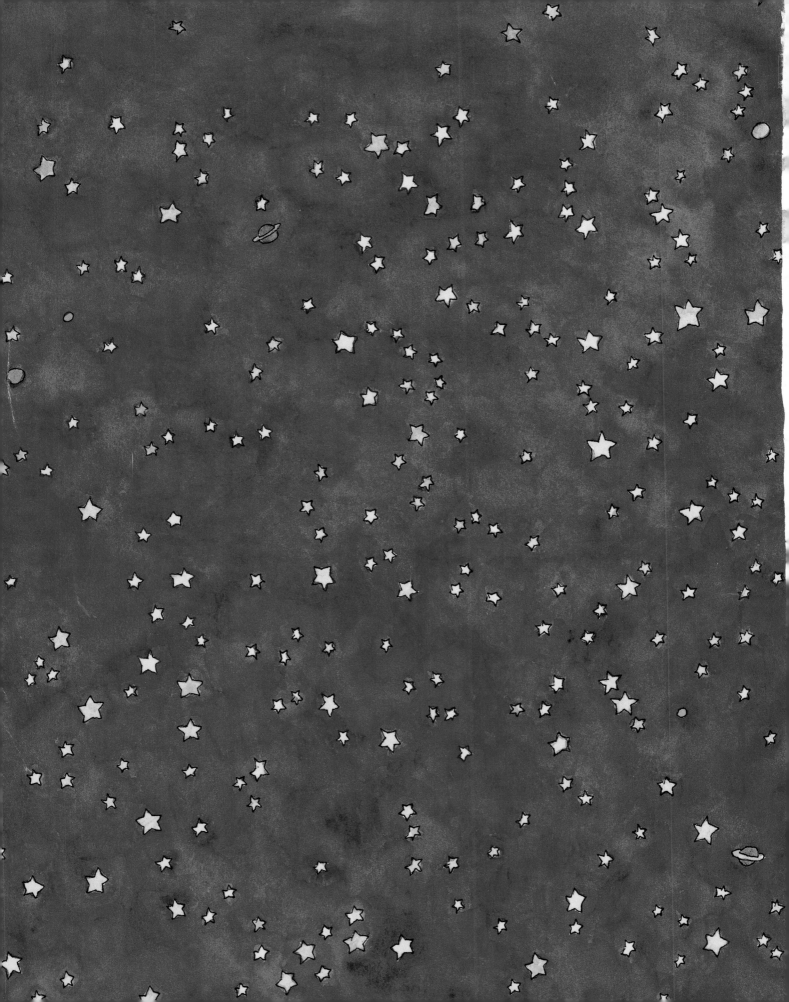

EARTHDANCE
by Lynn Reiser

Greenwillow Books, New York

Watercolor paints and a black pen were used for the full-color art.
The text type is Futura Bold.
Copyright © 1999 by Lynn Whisnant Reiser.
Page 32 constitutes an extension of this copyright page.
Greenwillow Books, a division of William Morrow & Company, Inc.,
1350 Avenue of the Americas, New York, NY 10019.
www.williammorrow.com   Printed in Singapore by Tien Wah Press
First Edition   10   9   8   7   6   5   4   3   2   1

Library of Congress Cataloging-in-Publication Data
Reiser, Lynn.   Earthdance / by Lynn Reiser
p.   cm.
Summary: As Terra performs her part in a school show
about the Earth and the solar system, her mother, who is an astronaut,
is hurrying back from space with a special ending for the production.
ISBN 0-688-16326-2 (trade). ISBN 0-688-16327-0 (lib. bdg.)
[1. Earth—Fiction.   2. Schools—Fiction.]   I. Title.
PZ7.R27745Ear   1999   [E]—dc21
98-41378   CIP   AC

For Suzy,
an urban astronaut

This is Terra.
She lives
in a house
in a town
in a country
on a continent
on the planet Earth.

This is Terra's father.
This is Terra's brother.

And this is Terra's mother.
Terra's mother
is an astronaut.

On the morning
of the school show,
Terra's mother
had to make
a quick trip
to the edge
of the universe.

She promised
to drive carefully,
not to dawdle,
and to remember
to bring back a picture
for the end
of Terra's show.

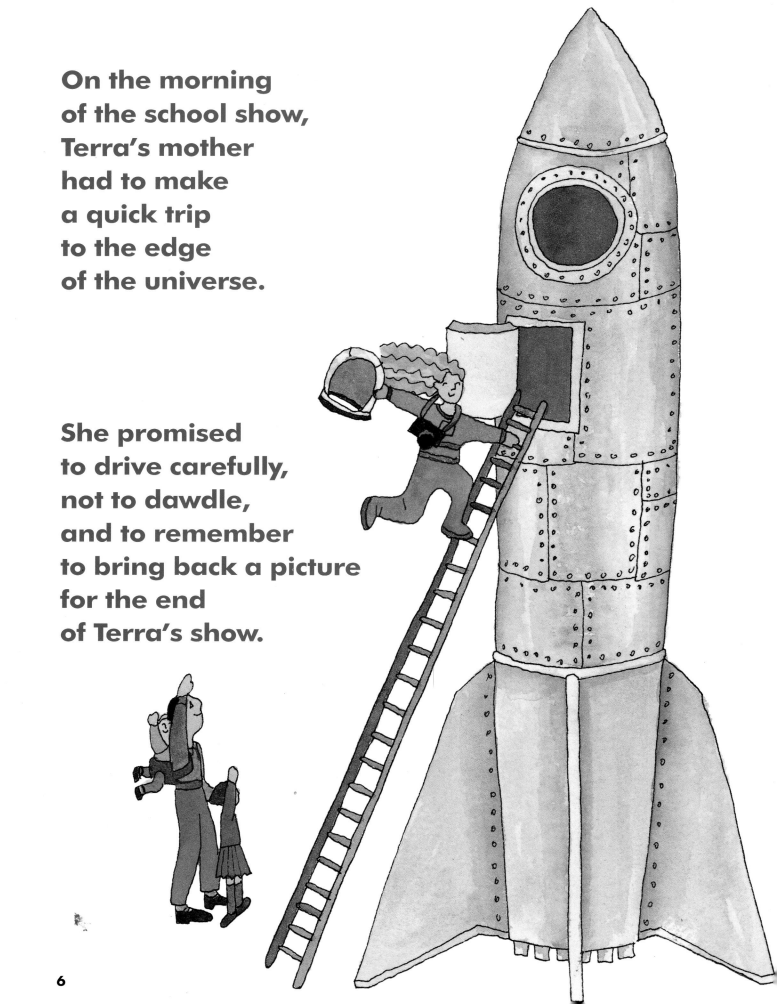

All morning
Terra's mother
traveled away.

All afternoon
she explored
the universe.

All morning and all afternoon
Terra practiced for the school show.

By the time
Terra's mother
fired up
the rockets
for the trip home,
it was evening.

The show
was about
to begin.

School Show
EARTHDANCE
TONIGHT

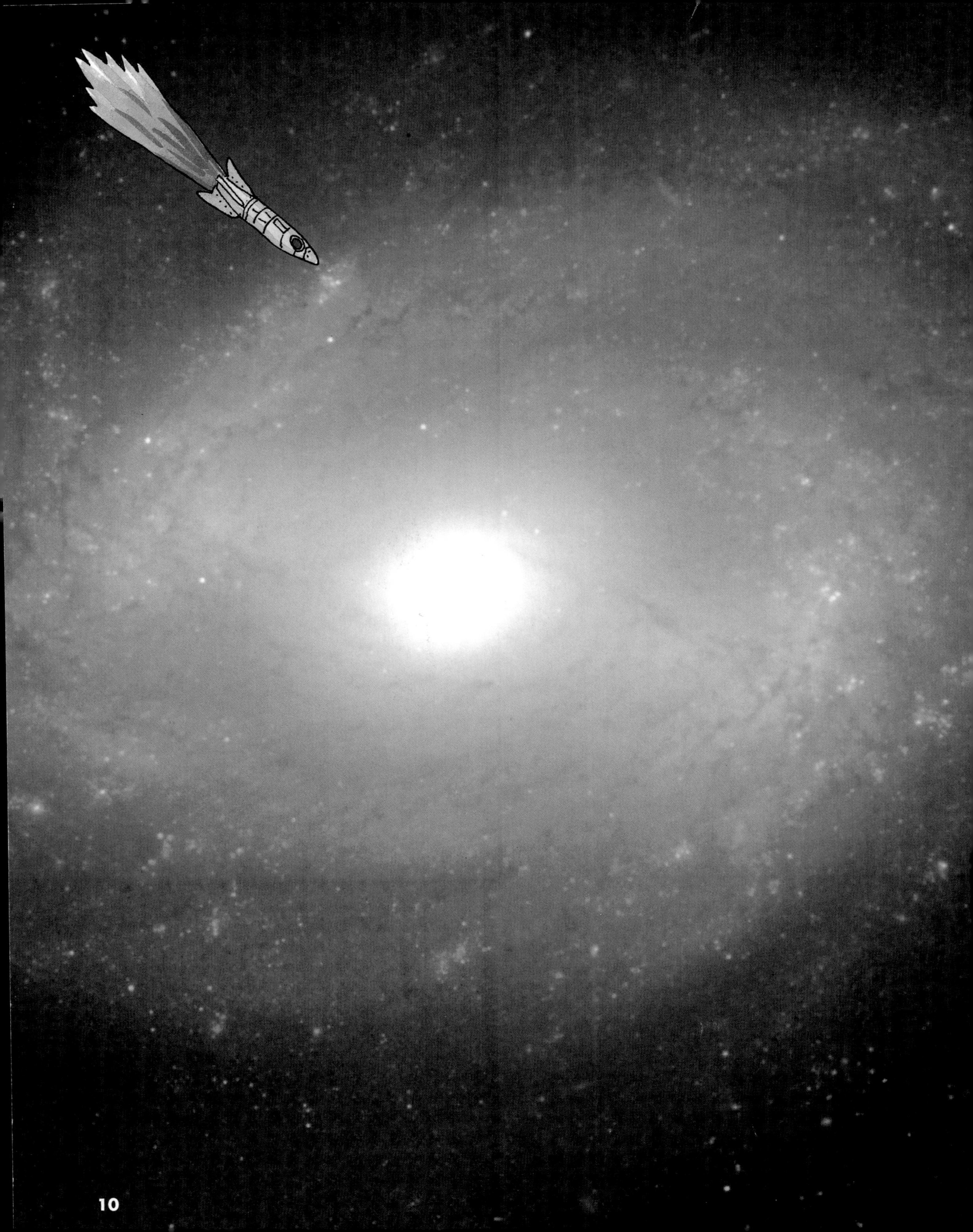

In the silent space
between the stars,

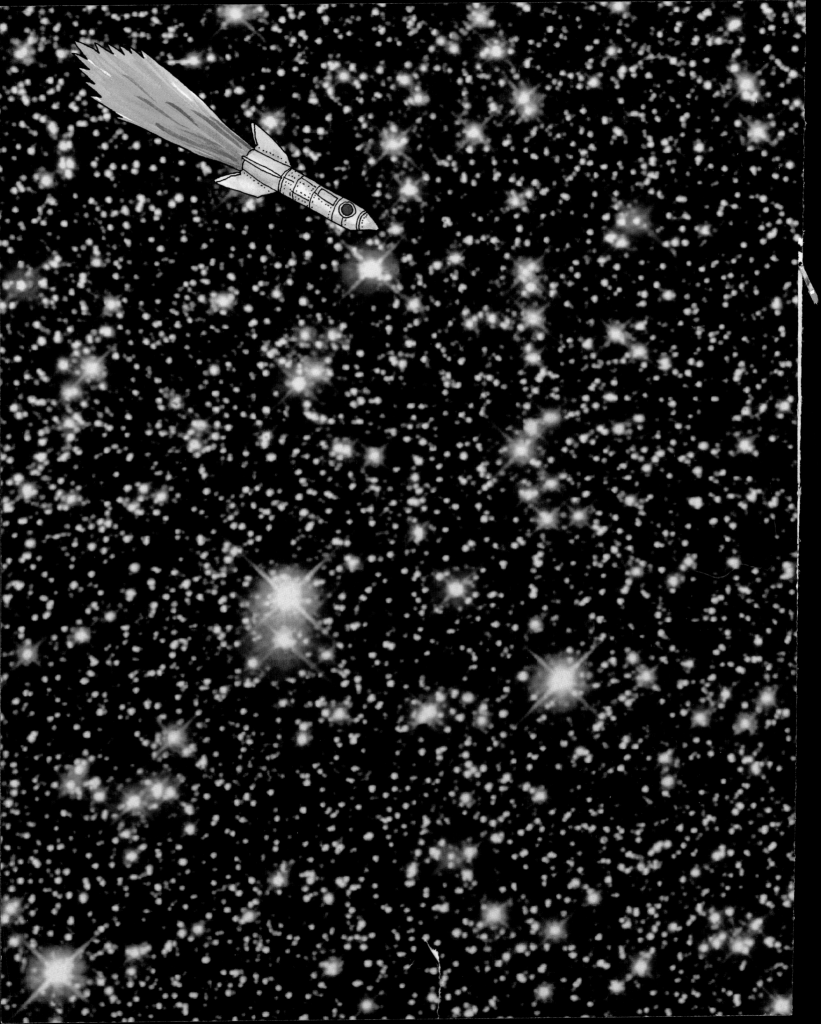

in the middle of the Milky Way,
the Earth dances.

Held in the circles
of the planets,

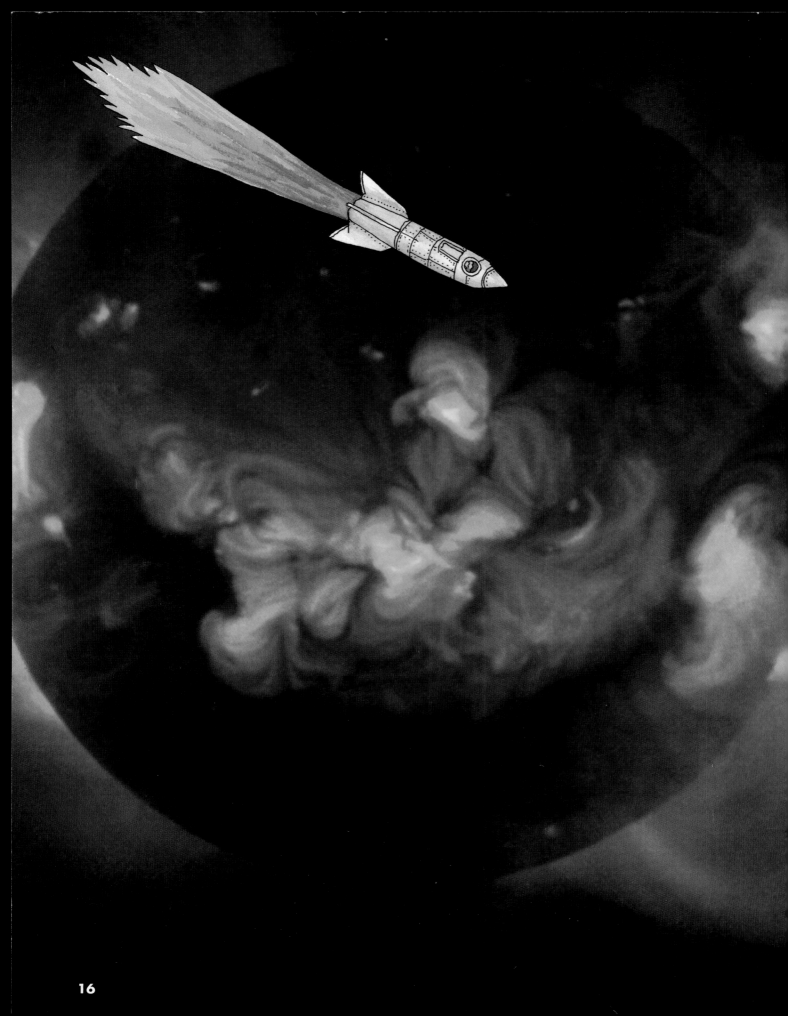

around her sun she turns,

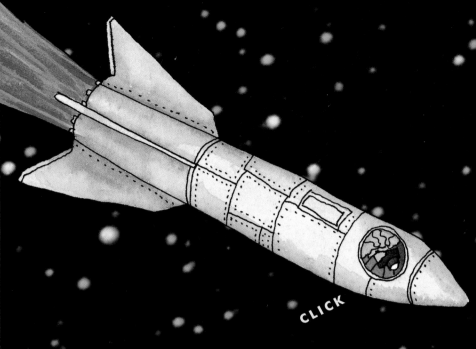

CLICK

and turns her moon.

Through the years she whirls,
tilting into summer, spinning into fall,
tipping into winter, twirling past spring.

Tilting, spinning, tipping, twirling,
the Earth turns
through the days into the nights.

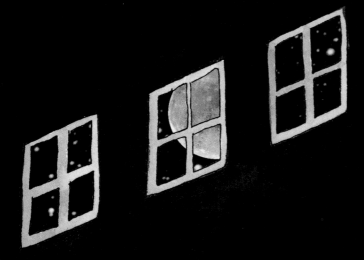

Sheltered, secured, we turn with her,
singing, sleeping, dancing, dreaming,
awake, asleep.

In the silent space between the stars,
the Earth dances.

That night,
after the school show,
tucked into her bed
in her house
in her town
in her country
on her continent
on her planet Earth,
Terra dreamed she was
an astronaut —

dancing.

The Aerospace Education Services Program of the National Aeronautics and Space Administration (NASA) provided the incredible photographs of space that are used in this book.

THE EARTH
Cover and pages 18 (right), 20 (lower right), 22 (lower left), 24 (center), 27 (twice), 32

This view of Earth is nicknamed "the marble." It was taken in December 1972 by the Apollo 17 crew as they traveled toward the Moon. *Credit: NASA*

NIGHT SKY
Cover and background of pages 18, 20, 22, 24, 26, 30, 32

This is a computer-enhanced image based on the background from a photograph of the Comet Hale-Bopp taken at the Jet Propulsion Laboratory Table Mountain Observatory. *Credit: NASA*

DEEP SPACE
Page 7 (twice)

This "deepest-ever" picture of the sky was assembled from 276 views made with the Hubble Space Telescope on ten days from December 18 to December 28, 1995.

Credit: Robert Williams and the Hubble Deep Field Team/ NASA

YOUNG GALAXY SURVEY
Page 8

This image was taken on September 4, 1996, with the Hubble Space Telescope.

Credit: Rogier Windhorst and Sam Pascarelle (Arizona State University) and NASA

A SPIRAL GALAXY LIKE THE MILKY WAY
Page 10

This view of Galaxy NGC 4639 dated May 9, 1996, was made with the Hubble Space Telescope. It shows a spiral galaxy located 78 million light-years away in the Virgo cluster of galaxies.

Credit: A. Sandage (Carnegie Observatories), A. Saha (STSE), G. A. Tammann and L. Labhardt (Astronomical Institute, University of Basel), F. D. Macchetto and N. Panagia (STSVESA), and NASA

SAGITTTARIUS STAR CLOUD
Page 12

This image of stars in the Milky Way was taken on October 21,1998, with the Hubble Space Telescope.

Credit: Hubble Heritage Team (AURA/STScl) and NASA

SOLAR SYSTEM LITHOGRAPH SET
Page 14

A schematic view of the planets—Mercury, Venus, Earth, Mars, Jupiter, Saturn, Uranus, Neptune, Pluto—that shows their size and position relative to the Sun. *Credit: NASA*

THE SUN
Page 16

This view of the sun was taken from space by the Soft X-Ray Telescope on the Japan/US/UK Yohkoh Mission on January 24, 1992. *Credit: NASA*

THE MOON
Page 18 (left), page 20 (top), page 22 (top), page 24 (top left), page 26 (top left), page 30 (top center)

This photograph of the Moon dated July 21, 1969, was taken from the Apollo 11 Spacecraft during its journey homeward. *Credit: NASA*

THE EARTH
Page 20 (right lower corner)

This view of Earth was taken on April 16, 1972, about one hour after translunar injection. *Credit: NASA*